JAMESTOWN SETTLEMENT

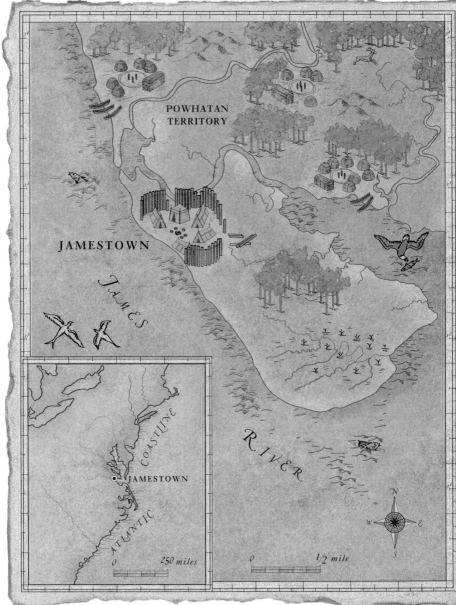

POWHATAN
TERRITORY

JAMESTOWN

JAMES

RIVER

JAMESTOWN

COASTLINE

ATLANTIC

0   250 miles

0   1/2 mile

N
W   E
S

Disney's POCAHONTAS

Little Mischief

by Leslie McGuire

Illustrations by Rachelle & Brooks Campbell,
Peter Emslie and D. Blakely Fuller

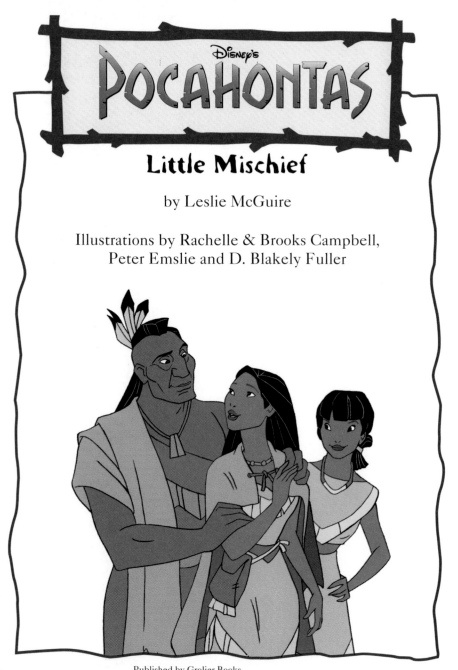

Published by Grolier Books.
©1995 The Walt Disney Company. No portion of this book may be reproduced without the consent of The Walt Disney Company.
Produced by Mega-Books, Inc.
Design and art direction by Michaelis/Carpelis Design Assoc., Inc.
Printed in the United States of America.

ISBN: 0-7172-8467-0

Grolier Books

CHAPTER 1

"Now what?" cried Nakoma. "It's freezing!"

"Just follow me," Pocahontas called over her shoulder. "I need goose feathers, and this is the only way to get good ones!"

It was a blustery late-fall day in 1605. Pocahontas and her friend Nakoma lived near a river that ran into the Chesapeake Bay.

Pocahontas wrapped her cloak around herself as she ran through the forest. The cold wind tugged at the edges.

"I can't believe you're doing this," Nakoma muttered. "Why feathers now? It's late, and it's going to rain any minute!"

"Hush. The geese will hear us."

Pocahontas looked back at the village. Lines of smoke rose from the holes on top of the houses on the edge of the forest. No one had seen them leave. She raced onto the bluff overlooking the great river with Nakoma behind her. The water surged against the rocks below.

Nakoma's bangs were being blown straight up by the stiff wind. "What mischief do you want these feathers for, anyhow?" she asked.

"I'm going to put them on a deerskin pouch as a present for my father."

The girls scrambled down a path that ran along the side of the bluff. They emerged onto a marsh that looked like a storm cloud. Hundreds of majestic gray and white geese were milling around and honking joyously.

Pocahontas ran right into the middle of the flock.

The geese rose into the air in a great mass of noise and feathers. Minutes later, Pocahontas was standing alone in the marsh with a few goose tail feathers clutched in each fist.

"Got 'em!" She tucked them into her waistband.

"Good! Can we leave now?" Nakoma asked as she started back up the path. She was already at the top when Pocahontas caught up, panting. But before Pocahontas could answer, she heard a wild laugh coming from the woods. In seconds, a small boy shot out onto the bluff.

"Oh! It's only you, Chamah," she said. Pocahontas looked closely at what he was waving over his head and gasped. "Where did you get that?"

Chamah was playing with a necklace. The copper ornament glinted as it flew around and around.

"You're not allowed to touch that!" Pocahontas cried.

"Why not?"

"Only chiefs are supposed to touch those necklaces," said Pocahontas. "Powhatan is the only one who can wear it!" Powhatan was Pocahontas's father and chief of the Powhatan Indians.

"But I found it," said the small boy. "Nobody was wearing it, so I figured nobody wanted it!"

"It's to be given as a gift to our neighbor, the Chowanoc chief, tomorrow," Nakoma said. "If it's missing, then the ceremony to keep our tribal friendship strong will be ruined."

"But we're already friends with the Chowanocs," said Chamah.

"But we stay friends by giving each other gifts," said Pocahontas. "The Chowanoc chief might be insulted."

"And you'll get into more trouble than you can even guess!" added Nakoma.

"Put it back before my father sees that it's missing," Pocahontas said. "We promise we won't tell on you."

"Soon," Chamah said. He danced over to the edge of the bluff. He tossed the necklace up high, then caught it by the leather thong.

"Hurry!" said Pocahontas. She started to walk toward the boy. "There's a storm coming. We have to get back home."

"See how well I can juggle?" Chamah yelled. He tossed the necklace even higher. His voice was almost lost in the roaring wind. "I bet I can—"

But he never finished the sentence. All three gasped as a gust of wind caught the copper ornament. Chamah grabbed for the necklace, but it flew over the edge of the bluff, then down and out of sight.

CHAPTER 2

Chamah rushed to the edge of the
bluff and looked over. All he could see
below was the foaming water crashing
against the rocks.

"I was going to take it back!" he cried.
"Now what will happen? I have to get it!"

Chamah whirled and scrambled down
the bluff.

"Wait!" shrieked Pocahontas, looking
at the darkening sky. "You can't . . ."

But Chamah didn't stop. Nakoma and

Pocahontas stared down at him. They had both seen the long line of black clouds moving toward them.

"We have to get away from the water!" Pocahontas screamed to Nakoma. "The storm is coming in faster than I thought!"

Chamah was already climbing out on the slippery rocks at the shore.

"He'll never find it!" cried Nakoma.

"He can't dive now!" shouted Pocahontas. "The current is too fast. He'll smash his head on the rocks."

But it was clear that Chamah was more afraid of what would happen if he didn't get the necklace back. The girls watched in horror as he jumped from the rocky shore into the water.

Pocahontas and Nakoma scrambled down the bluff and onto the rocks just in time to see Chamah's head pop out of the water. His teeth were chattering, and he was sobbing.

"I can't see anything," he cried. "I'll

never get the necklace back. What will happen to me?"

The girls had no answer for him. Chamah dived down two more times. But each time he came up empty-handed. Finally Chamah climbed out of the water. Pocahontas quickly wrapped the boy in her cloak. He was shaking so hard, it seemed to her that he might fall.

"I can't go back," he said. "Not until I find the necklace!"

"You have to go back," Pocahontas said. "You'll freeze to death if you don't get into some warm clothes."

"We'll look later," Nakoma promised.

Chamah tore off the cloak. "No! Leave me alone!"

He turned and raced up the path to the top of the bluff. Pocahontas and Nakoma ran after him, but by the time they reached the top, he was gone.

"He probably went home," Nakoma said thoughtfully.

"We'd better go back, too," said Pocahontas as she put her cloak around her shoulders. "The rain will start any moment. I bet he's already back home by the fire."

When they got to the village, they searched for Chamah. He wasn't back yet.

"Ah, there you are!" Powhatan cried when Pocahontas slipped into the house. "A terrible storm is coming. Where have you been?"

Pocahontas felt for the goose feathers in her waistband. Good. Her cloak hid them from view.

"Oh, just out, er, with Nakoma."

Her father looked at her closely, a frown creasing his forehead. "We didn't give you a name that meant Little Mischief for nothing. What have you been up to?"

Pocahontas smiled, trying to look innocent.

"Just stay inside," Powhatan said, sighing heavily. "It's a dangerous night, and you need to help the women prepare food for tomorrow's ceremony."

"But, Father, I have to—"

"There's too much work to be done," Powhatan said. "I don't want to hear any arguments. You're old enough to stop thinking about games all the time."

Pocahontas lowered her head. There was no point in arguing. She made her way to the baskets of corn and acorns tucked against the far wall of the house.

With her back to her father, she shoved the feathers into a leather bag. Then she took off her cloak and pulled out the mill-stones. She poured a scoopful of corn into the hollowed surface of one stone. She picked up the other, a long oval stone, and started to grind the dried kernels into flour.

Nakoma came in just as Powhatan was leaving.

"Nakoma, you will help Pocahontas grind the corn," he said. "And also make sure she doesn't run off someplace!"

As soon as he was gone, Pocahontas hissed, "Did you find Chamah? Is he home yet?"

"No," whispered Nakoma. "I think he ran away. Otherwise, why isn't he back?"

"We have to find him!"

"No. We should tell someone."

"We can't," said Pocahontas. "He'll get into too much trouble. I'll go find him myself!"

"But there's a horrible storm coming!" Nakoma said. "Your father has forbidden you to leave!"

"I don't care." Pocahontas grabbed her cloak and the leather bag. "I'm sure Chamah's hiding close by. I'll be right back."

"No! You can't . . . " Nakoma cried. But Pocahontas was gone.

CHAPTER 3

Pocahontas pushed out through the door flap of the house and looked around. Her father was nowhere in sight. The winds were whipping the tree branches back and forth. Everyone else in the tribe was inside. The coast was clear!

Pocahontas made a run for the edge of the forest. She didn't stop until she knew she was out of sight. Then she turned and looked back. She'd made it without being spotted by anyone!

Pocahontas sprinted down the path. She was trying to think of all the hiding places the village children used. She was sure Chamah was safe in one of them. And the hiding places were all close by.

She was also wondering how to get Chamah to come home. He hadn't known how important the necklace was. After all, he was a little boy, and losing it had been an accident. Pocahontas and Nakoma would both stick up for him, and he wouldn't get into too much trouble.

As Pocahontas raced through the woods, the tree branches whipped at her face. But, lost in her thoughts, she didn't notice. She also didn't notice that she was being followed.

A ball of gray fur shot out onto the path in front of her. She was so startled, she almost tripped on a root. Catching her balance, she just missed colliding with a tiny squeaking bird.

"Meeko!" she said to the raccoon

planted in her way. "Where did you come from? You should be in your nice dry den!"

Meeko tugged at her cloak. He was trying to get Pocahontas to turn back.

"Let go! And Flit . . . just stop it!" she said, laughing at the hummingbird that continued to fly around her head. "Go away! Leave me alone!"

Flit caught hold of her hair and tried to pull her back to the village.

"Stop acting so worried!" Pocahontas pulled Meeko's fingers loose and stepped over him. "I know there's a storm, but I won't go back until I've found Chamah. He should be right around here, so help me look for him."

Meeko and Flit looked at each other.

"Come along," said Pocahontas. She scooped Flit out of the air and set him on her shoulder. "It's too windy for you to fly," she said. "If we look together, we'll find him in two shakes of a hummingbird's tail!"

Meeko raced after Pocahontas and Flit. Howling winds whipped branches around like angry spirits. Leaving the path, Pocahontas dashed behind trees, into gullies, and over small rises. A branch crashed to the ground behind them. Meeko could barely keep up.

As Pocahontas raced from hiding place to hiding place, she was certain she would find Chamah. But she was getting farther and farther from the village.

A blinding flash of lightning lit up the entire forest. A second later, the booming explosion of a thunderclap almost knocked Pocahontas down. Then a huge tree in front of her gave a mighty crack and started to fall.

Pocahontas screamed and ran back. The tree just missed her. In seconds, the sky opened up. Sheets of drenching rain poured down.

Pocahontas couldn't see a thing. For the first time, she felt frightened.

Then another crack of lightning came. Another tree shuddered and fell. All around Pocahontas, heavy branches were crashing to the ground. The wind blew harder, and the pelting rain blinded her. Meeko squeaked as he dodged falling branches, and Flit huddled against Pocahontas's neck.

Pocahontas wasn't sure how far she was from the village. Even worse, she had lost her bearings. She had no idea which direction she should follow to get home.

"Uh-oh," Pocahontas said to a wet and miserable Meeko, "I hope we're not as lost as I think we are!" Tripping over fallen tree trunks and dodging wind-whipped branches, she stumbled on.

"Poca . . . hontas! Poca . . . hontas!"

Pocahontas snapped her head around. Who was calling her? She didn't see anything but a small river.

"Poca . . . hontas! Come to me . . . ."

The voice sounded like wind whistling

in the trees. Perhaps that's all it is, she thought, spinning around to find the owner of the voice.

"Chamah! Of course. That's who's calling," she cried as she ran toward the riverbank. "Finally I've found you!"

But when she got to the water's edge, there was no one there.

That's when she heard the distant howling of wolves.

CHAPTER
4

Pocahontas, Meeko, and Flit were alone in the darkness. Pocahontas was cold and wet. She knew she'd never find her way back to the village. And the howling wolves were coming closer.

Flit clung to her shoulder. He was jammed up against her ear, making little chittering noises. Meeko was a bedraggled ball of fur at her feet. Pocahontas had to think of a way to save them all.

Just then, the whispering voice she'd

been hearing floated through the wind and rain.

"Look up," it whispered. "Look up the river, Poca . . . hontas."

Pocahontas looked along the riverbank and saw the gnarled trunk and branches of an ancient willow tree. The huge roots of the tree swelled in clumps that came almost to Pocahontas's feet.

"Haven't you learned to come in out of the rain yet?" said the voice with a chuckle.

"Is that you, Grandmother Willow?" cried Pocahontas. "I can't believe I've come this far."

Pocahontas had found her way to the Enchanted Glade, where the wise spirit of the willow tree lived. Grandmother Willow had been a guiding friend to Pocahontas's mother and grandmother.

"Come quickly, child," said Grandmother Willow. "Hide safely in my roots. You cannot look for your friend tonight."

"How did you know . . . " Pocahontas

began as she ran toward the base of the tree.

"Shelter first, questions later," said Grandmother Willow. "Now, watch this!"

As Pocahontas stared, an orange glow appeared between two of the largest roots. At first, it was just a crack. But the crack became wider and wider. The earth at the base of Grandmother Willow was splitting open!

Unable to believe her eyes, Pocahontas bent closer. What she saw was a burrow swelling open under the roots of the tree. It was filled with a warm light the color of sunrise.

"Don't stand there all night, dear," said Grandmother Willow. "Come inside!"

Pocahontas scooped Meeko up in her arms and walked to the opening. She had to crouch down to get into the burrow.

Meeko's eyes were wide with wonder. But Flit zoomed off Pocahontas's shoulder and darted from one side to the other.

"It's dry in here!" Pocahontas exclaimed, not believing what she was seeing. "It's like magic."

"Yes, it is, isn't it?" said Grandmother Willow. "I've always loved that trick!"

Pocahontas shivered.

"Oh, my dear," said Grandmother Willow with a little chuckle. "What you need is a fire."

Pocahontas realized she was right. She looked around and saw the burrow was filled with dry leaves, twigs, branches, and pieces of bark. She made a small pile of twigs and scraps of bark on the floor. On top, she placed a cone-shaped pile of twigs. Then she began twirling a stick against a piece of bark.

Pocahontas had often seen the village medicine man do this. But she'd never paid very close attention. Now she wished she had.

"Pocahontas, that's taking too long," said Grandmother Willow. "You are

almost dry now, but I can see you are still cold. Here, let me help."

A glowing coal appeared inside the cone of twigs. It grew brighter for a second, then the leaves caught. Soon a small fire was crackling away.

Meeko and Flit watched, fascinated, as Pocahontas collected some big sheets of bark and used them to block the opening against the wind. Then she made a bed out of the dry leaves. As the storm howled outside, Pocahontas curled herself into the bed.

After a few moments, Pocahontas sat up and pulled the goose feathers from the leather bag. Meeko snuggled next to her, and Flit settled himself on her shoulder.

"I'd better work on this pouch for Father," said Pocahontas. "There's nothing else to do, and perhaps if I bring him a present, he won't be so angry."

But Pocahontas didn't realize how tired she was. Her eyes slowly closed, and soon she was fast asleep.

What felt like seconds later, Pocahontas heard howling, but this time, it sounded as if it were right outside the burrow.

Sitting up with a jerk, Pocahontas realized she'd been asleep for a long time. The fire was just embers. With trembling hands, she got the fire blazing again. But the voices of the wolves surrounded the tree. They were on all sides, circling. "Why don't they attack?" she whispered. "Are they afraid of fire?"

Pocahontas knew wolves rarely attacked people. But if they were hungry enough, they sometimes did.

"Do not fall asleep again," whispered Grandmother Willow. "You must keep the fire going—no matter what!"

CHAPTER 5

Pocahontas collected more twigs to keep the fire going. She was tired, but she pulled a piece of deerskin and some shells out of her bag and started to work.

First she showed Meeko where to bite holes in the deerskin to make the lacing easier. Then she tore a few long, thin strips off the edge of her cloak to use for laces.

"This should help me stay awake, right, Meeko?" she said with a yawn. But her eyes kept trying to close.

"Oh, dear," said Pocahontas when she laid out the feathers. "I need one more. But it's too late now!"

Flit, who had been darting around watching, landed at her feet. Craning his head, he grabbed a tail feather and yanked it out.

"Why, thank you," said Pocahontas as he set his own feather down next to the others. "That's perfect for my design."

Pocahontas worked on the pouch till she was finished. The howling of the wolves had stopped. That made it even harder to keep her eyes open. But Grandmother Willow's whispered words kept ringing in her ears.

"Do not fall asleep again. You must keep the fire going—no matter what!"

Then she heard a sharp digging noise outside. In seconds, Pocahontas was wide awake. Something was trying to get into the burrow.

Pocahontas picked up one of the

biggest sticks. She raised it over her head and crawled toward the opening. The wind was roaring outside, and she heard the crash of another tree falling to the earth. Meeko, trembling, was right behind her. Flit was perched on her shoulder.

Just as she got to the opening, the bark door fell over with a crash. Pocahontas scrambled back. But what she saw was nothing to be afraid of. It was a tiny wolf pup. As soon as the pup felt the warmth of the fire, he staggered into the burrow whimpering, then collapsed. Meeko sniffed the pup while Flit hovered close to his small, wet head.

"You poor little thing!" murmured Pocahontas. She reached for the pup. That's when she saw the blood.

"Oh, my! You're hurt," she said gently.

The pup didn't move, but he whimpered again softly as Pocahontas examined him to see what was wrong. She found a gash on the pup's right foreleg.

The pup flinched when she touched it.

"Uh-oh," Pocahontas whispered. "This isn't good. And you're in pain. What am I going to do with you?"

The pup licked her hand.

"Have you forgotten everything you know about healing?" Grandmother Willow asked. "Look around you. Everything you need is here."

Pocahontas rested her hand gently on the pup's heaving rib cage as she looked around the burrow. She saw willow bark. She saw cobwebs.

Grandmother Willow was right. Everything she needed was here. Pocahontas knew that the bark of the willow tree was a painkiller. She would give the pup a piece of bark to chew on. But in the meantime, she had to stop the pup's leg from bleeding.

Pocahontas collected some of the cobwebs and a few pieces of willow bark. She gently patted the cobwebs onto the wound. Then she peeled off some soft inner bark and wrapped it like a bandage around the pup's leg, tying it loosely with a length of vine. At last, she carried the pup over to the fire and gave him a piece of bark. Snuggling against Pocahontas's side, he chewed sleepily on the bark until he fell asleep.

"That was perfect, dear," said Grandmother Willow. "You did all the right things. You saved the pup's life."

"Thank you for reminding me of what I know," said Pocahontas. "And thank you for telling me to keep the fire going. The fire led the pup to this safe place."

"Now it is safe for you to sleep," Grandmother Willow whispered softly.

Though she fell asleep with Meeko, Flit, and the pup, Pocahontas didn't feel safe. The pup was the reason the wolves had been circling the burrow. They were searching for their lost young one. She knew they would return.

CHAPTER 6

Morning dawned clear and cold. At first, Pocahontas couldn't remember where she was. But then, as she looked around her and felt the wolf pup at her side, everything that had happened the day before came flooding back.

She had been lost in a terrifying storm. Now she was safe in a magical burrow under Grandmother Willow's roots. Still, wolves were looking for this lost pup. And she had not found poor Chamah. Today was the day of the ceremony. Her father would be terribly worried because she hadn't come home last night. Nakoma would be in trouble for letting her leave. Chamah would be in trouble for losing the necklace.

Even worse, Pocahontas would be in big, big trouble for disobeying her father—that is, she would be if she ever made it home.

Pocahontas put more wood on the embers. Soon the fire was blazing again.

"Are you feeling any better, little one?" she asked the pup, who was following her every move. She began to pet the pup. He licked her hand.

Pocahontas wrapped clean bark around the pup's foreleg. The wound looked much better this morning, and there was no bleeding.

Pocahontas poured dirt onto the fire to put it out and picked up the pouch she had made. At least something was done right, she thought. She placed the pouch in her bag and crawled out of the burrow. The pup followed her. Meeko and Flit stuck their noses out of the opening.

"We need to get home," Pocahontas said. But as she looked around, she saw a devastated forest. Trees were down, some leaning against each other. Broken branches littered the ground as far as she could see. How could she get her bearings?

"The river is still here," she said to Meeko. "We'll follow it until we can see smoke from the village to guide us."

And that's when she felt she was being watched. Pocahontas scanned the clearing but saw nothing unusual. Then she looked back at Grandmother Willow.

A face started to form in the folds and whorls of the bark. Two crinkled eyes, a strong nose, and a mouth that widened into a smile appeared.

Pocahontas gasped. "I've never seen your face before, Grandmother Willow," she said. "I've always known you were there for me because my mother told me so . . . but I didn't know that I could see you as well as hear you!"

"You weren't quite old enough, my dear," said Grandmother Willow. "Your mischief was just child's play. But last night, your mischief got you into some very grown-up trouble. It was time for me to show myself. Besides, it was such a pleasure to have a guest."

"I'm afraid I'll need more help to get home," Pocahontas said.

"The spirits will guide you," said Grandmother Willow. "I am part of nature, as you and all living things are. We are all part of the world, and we work in harmony. Nature speaks to you in many different ways."

"What ways?" asked Pocahontas.

"Well, for example," said Grandmother Willow, "the wolf pup is a sign to you from nature. Like the wolf, you have a wild,

free heart. Nature is telling you to trust your instincts because they are good."

"I'm in a lot of trouble for following my instincts."

"The spirits know this, but they also know that you get into trouble because freedom is not enough. Like the wolf pup, you must discover that the other side of freedom is discipline. If you listen to your own voice alone, there can be no harmony, no safety. Your wisdom will lead you to honor the voice of your people as the pup must honor the will of his pack."

"That's just the way my mother's mother used to talk," said Pocahontas. "She was one of the wisest women in the tribe."

"And so shall you be wise, as well," said Grandmother Willow. "Now it is time for the spirits to guide you home."

Pocahontas heard a rustling in the forest, and her heart filled with terror. The clearing was filling with wolves!

CHAPTER 7

"Oh, no!" murmured Pocahontas as she watched more and more wolves glide out of the forest. "There are so many of them!"

Meeko and Flit pulled back into the burrow as the wolves formed a quiet circle around the willow tree. They filled the entire clearing. They were all watching Pocahontas.

Pocahontas was about to join Meeko and Flit when the pup yelped. All eyes

stared at the pup as he raced toward the wolves. The pack was watching the way the little wolf ran without a limp.

A small adult wolf stepped out of the ring of wolves as the pup skidded to a stop.

That must be the mother, Pocahontas thought. She watched as the she-wolf joyously nuzzled her pup.

The mother licked her baby. She sniffed him all over, checking his scent. The cub had spent the night with a human girl. Obviously, Pocahontas thought, his mother needed to make sure he had not been harmed.

After she had sniffed at the leg wrapped in willow bark, the she-wolf raised her head to look at Pocahontas. Then, very slowly, as if she knew she might frighten the human girl by moving too fast, the wolf walked towards her. Pocahontas froze. She watched the wolf come closer and closer, but she could not move her feet to run away. When the wolf reached her, she stopped and licked Pocahontas's hand. Meeko and Flit slowly came out of the burrow.

"You see, the wolves trust you," said Grandmother Willow. "You have helped them by caring for one of their children. Now you must trust them in return."

Pocahontas stretched her hands out. One by one, the wolves came forward to lick her hands and accept a pat on the head. By this time, Meeko and Flit were chattering with excitement. They were still worried. But as they watched the procession of wolves greet Pocahontas, they grew braver.

Flit swooped out into the clearing and flew over the wolves' heads. Meeko, inspired by Flit's courage, came out too. The little pup raced over to Meeko and gave him a big, wet kiss on the nose.

But soon the biggest wolf in the pack walked to the edge of the clearing. He raised his head and gave a long, low howl.

"It is time," said Grandmother Willow. "The wolves will show you the way home. You must follow them."

Pocahontas watched as the pack started to move through the trees. Then she turned back to her friend.

"Thank you for everything, Grandmother Willow," Pocahontas said. "For saving my life last night, and for teaching me so much."

"It was my pleasure, dear," said Grandmother Willow. "And just in case you're interested, I didn't teach you anything. I just reminded you of what you already know."

"I'll miss you," Pocahontas said sadly.

"Why is that?" asked Grandmother Willow with a laugh. "Aren't you going to visit me again?"

Pocahontas's eyes opened wide, and then she laughed, too. "Of course. I'll be back as soon as I can. But it may take a while for my father to let me out of the village after this. I may not even be allowed out of the house!"

"I'll expect you whenever you are able to come," said Grandmother Willow. There was a twinkle in her eyes. "After all, I'm not going anyplace."

Pocahontas laughed. She leaned forward and kissed the rough bark on Grandmother Willow's cheek. Then she waved and ran to catch up with the wolf pack.

They headed through the forest quickly. Soon Pocahontas saw ribbons of smoke above the treetops.

"That's it!" she cried. "I'm home!"

The wolves led her up a rise, and she could look down onto the village and see people rushing all over. They were busy preparing for the friendship ceremony.

Pocahontas turned to the pack.

"I'll be fine now," she said, reaching down to pet the pup. "Be careful little one. Listen to your mother. Otherwise, you'll make too much mischief and always be in trouble—just like me!"

The pup licked Pocahontas's hand as the she-wolf nuzzled her leg. Then the pack melted silently into the forest.

Pocahontas took a deep breath. She was not looking forward to the welcome she was going to get. Once her father saw she was safe, he was going to be very, very angry indeed.

But there was nothing she could do about it.

"Wish me luck!" she whispered to Meeko and Flit. Then she ran down to the village.

CHAPTER 8

Pocahontas skidded down the sunlit slope. It was muddy from the storm of the previous night. After landing in a small puddle at the edge of the village, she quickly made her way behind the huts.

Everywhere villagers were carrying baskets, grinding acorns, and bending over fires stirring pots. Spits were turning in front of every house, and the smell of roasting venison and fowl made Pocahontas's mouth water.

The villagers were wearing their best fringed mantles decorated with shells and small mussel pearls. Their necks were draped with shell necklaces and feathered chains. Even the little ones had face and body paint that gleamed in the morning light.

Pocahontas wondered whether Chamah had returned. Had her father discovered that the copper necklace was missing? If so, she hoped Nakoma had managed to keep Chamah from being punished too harshly. And that reminded her of her father's anger.

Pocahontas crept along the side of her father's house, hoping no one would see her. Then, quick as a fox, she pulled aside the flap covering the doorway and slipped inside.

And there sat Powhatan, his head in his hands. He was not dressed for the ceremony yet. He hadn't even applied his body paint. Hearing the rustle at the door-

way, Powhatan barely moved.

"Who is it?" he asked slowly. Then he looked up. His face was filled with sadness, the lines deeper than usual. "My child!" he boomed, leaping to his feet. "What happened? Where were you? Are you safe? Are you hurt?"

"I'm so sorry, Father," Pocahontas mumbled as he swept her into a bear hug.

"We thought you had been hurt!" said Powhatan, holding her at arm's length. "What happened? The search party has been looking for you all night!"

"Well, I went looking for Chamah . . ." she began.

Powhatan scowled. "Chamah returned last night."

"Is he all right? He was afraid of being punished because he—"

"Yes, yes, yes," said Powhatan. "We know all about it. Chamah is just as mischievous as you are. He found the necklace he so stupidly lost. It was caught on a bush halfway down the bluff. But what does that have to do with you? You were forbidden to leave the house."

Powhatan's face looked like the previous day's storm clouds as Pocahontas began to tell her story.

"Chamah was lost, but that is no excuse," he said. "You should have told the elders. In this tribe, the men are the ones who look for a lost child. Girls should not go into the woods alone at night. There are too many dangers, my child. There are wolves out there!"

"But that's what I've been trying to tell you," sputtered Pocahontas. "So many things happened!"

Powhatan was silent as she told him of her meeting with Grandmother Willow and how she saved the wolf pup and how the wolves helped her find her way home.

"You are so much like your mother." Powhatan sighed. "It's a good thing that Grandmother Willow is here to help me raise you, Little Mischief."

"Grandmother Willow reminded me of all the things I already know," said Pocahontas softly.

"Well, it seems that you received a powerful lesson from the spirits last night," Powhatan said gravely. "That does not excuse your behavior. But you have been given an important gift."

Pocahontas bowed her head. Her stomach growled with hunger. She expected her father would next say she would not be allowed to attend the ceremony or eat any of the delicious food she could smell cooking. But he didn't.

"The wolf is the spirit of freedom," he said. "Just like you."

"I know, Father," said Pocahontas. "That's just what Grandmother Willow said."

Powhatan nodded.

"But the wolves mean more than just freedom," Pocahontas went on. "They also understand discipline and loyalty. They always obey the rules of the pack, for that is where their strength lies. The wolves know that there must be a balance between the wishes of one creature and the protection and safety of the group. It is the balance between rules and freedom. Maybe they taught me this lesson because I helped save their pup."

"Exactly," said Powhatan. "That's why they decided to help you. But more important, since you were so kind, they accepted you as one of their children. That means the wolf spirit will always guard you as it teaches you. And it will teach you with love."

"And I will do my best to learn, Father," Pocahontas said softly. Then she reached into her bag and brought out the pouch. "I have a gift for you . . . ."

Powhatan looked at the pouch and started to laugh. "You think a present might make me less angry?"

Pocahontas lowered her eyes. "Well . . . " she began.

Nakoma burst into the house. "I heard you were back!" she cried. "What happened?"

"It's a long story," said Powhatan, taking a deep breath. "It always is, with Little Mischief. But you'll hear it later. Right now, let's get something to eat. After all, there's a celebration about to begin!"